For Dad, in loving memory;
and for Aunt P, whose cobbler was beyond compare.
—G.D.

To the memory of my grandmother Vivian, who taught
me everything I know about cooking. And to my
family and friends, who reap the benefits of those lessons.
—K.H.

The illustrations for this book were made with
digital acrylic and pencil.

Cataloging-in-Publication Data has been applied for
and may be obtained from the Library of Congress.

ISBN 978-1-4197-5737-2

Text © 2024 Gabriele Davis
Illustrations © 2024 Kim Holt
Book design by Heather Kelly

Printed and bound in China
10 9 8 7 6 5 4 3 2 1

Abrams Books for Young Readers are available at special discounts when purchased in quantity for premiums
and promotions as well as fundraising or educational use. Special editions can also be created to specification.
For details, contact specialsales@abramsbooks.com or the address below.

ABRAMS The Art of Books
195 Broadway, New York, NY 10007
abramsbooks.com

Peaches

Written by
GABRIELE DAVIS

Illustrated by
KIM HOLT

Abrams Books for Young Readers

New York

Summer Sundays begin with picking. With me and Grandma, straw hats tilted to tease the sun, walking side by side into our orchard. Rosy-ripe peaches dipping low to the ground, sun-warmed and soft like Grandma's lap.

We pick and pick and pick some more, snatching and snapping 'til our buckets are full.

And sometimes we bite.
Peach juice drip,
drip,
dripping, down our chins, over our hands,
trickling down our arms. Soft pulp sliding down
our throats like honey. Grandma's sweet-tart
laugh hugging the air.

"Tastes like summer," she says.

Soon, Grandma fills up the house with sweetness. Daddy breathes deep and smiles. Smiles and then sighs, for the memory of Mama.

His peachy peach girl.

Arms hugging Daddy on new-home steps, fingers lacing, cheek pressing cheek . . .

Standing windblown and wild beneath our mighty oak . . .

Crimping peach cobbler crust, belly round, face aglow. Daddy leaning close-close, eyes smiling.

I look at Daddy then, and Daddy today.
His smile different now. Happy touched
with sad. Stopping at the edges of his
smooth, brown cheeks.

Mama left us when I was a sweet babe, a rock-me-in-her-arms-and-kiss-
my-cheek babe. I barely knew her, but I carry her in my heart. We all do.

"Grandma," I say, low so Daddy can't hear. "Teach me? Like you did Mama?"

Afternoon finds me hauling my bucket to Grandma's house. Huffing and puffing. Puffing and huffing. Spilling laughter as peaches spill onto her table.

Grandma's sure hands guide mine.

A pinch of this, a fistful of that.

Tossing, stirring, mixing, kneading.

"Once you learn the *feel* of making something," she says, "you never forget."

Next Sunday, when Daddy slips out for his morning run, I'm ready.

I set down my bucket and say, "Just me, Grandma. I got this."

But right off, things get messy.
Peaches roll. Drop. Squish.
Pressing in butter is hard, hard,
and my fingers hurt.
Then eggshells shatter, and bits slip in!

I pray the rest will be easy.
But dough grabs at the
counter, snatches at the roller,
and clumps up my fingers,
pulling tears from my eyes like
hot rain in a summer storm.

I want to give up and call Grandma in from the garden. But Daddy says when you've got a plan, you do your best to see it through.

I breathe deep. Then I remember the feel of flour sifting through my fingers . . .

The air is thick and sweet when I hear church bells ringing down the road.
A sure sign Daddy's almost home.

I hurry, hurry to mop up my mess. But I'm too slow. The screen door squeaks . . .

. . . and there's Daddy, standing tall, eyes wide. Seeing *me* where he expects Grandma will be.

Daddy smiles so big I think his face will break open. Then he hugs me, peach juice and all, and whispers, "Thank you."

Grandma tells me I'm just like Mama, warm and sweet, like the cobbler that conjures her memory. That Mama lives in me. And I know she's right.

Then Daddy laughs, face beaming, hand firm across my back.
And I know he lives in me, too. All of us together. Strong,
sweet, wild, proud. Seeing things through.

Now *I* make peach cobbler on summer Sundays. Peachy Peach, Peach Perfect. And Daddy and Grandma help. Side by side by side. Buckets swinging, Daddy humming. Feet whispering on our well-worn path.

Peaches hanging like little
suns in a leaf-green sky.

PEACH COBBLER

Ask an adult to help you make your own yummy peach cobbler.

WHAT YOU NEED

- 4 cups sliced peaches (fresh, frozen, or canned)
- 1 tablespoon fresh lemon juice
- ¼ cup sugar (slightly less if using canned peaches)
- ½ teaspoon nutmeg
- 1½ cups instant biscuit mix
- ½ cup milk
- ¼ cup butter, melted
- 1 egg
- ¼ teaspoon cinnamon + 1 tablespoon sugar, mixed (optional)

WHAT YOU DO

1. Preheat oven to 350°F. If you are using canned peaches, drain them. If frozen, allow to thaw.

2. Mix peaches, lemon juice, sugar, and nutmeg together in a large bowl. Pour into 8-inch-square baking dish.

3. Mix biscuit mix, milk, egg, and melted butter together to make a thick batter. Drop batter by the spoonful over the peaches. Sprinkle with cinnamon sugar (if desired).

4. Bake at 350°F for 30 to 40 minutes, or until bubbly and golden brown. Remove from oven and let sit for 10 minutes before serving. Top with vanilla ice cream for extra yumminess.

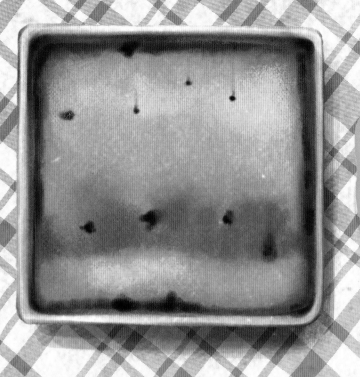